W9-BXY-809

A PLUME BOOK

T-REX TRYING AND TRYING

DR. HUGH MURPHY graduated from dental school at the University of Southern California and is currently in his residency at UNC Chapel Hill for advanced prosthodontics. He loves drawing, painting, fly-fishing, nature programs, and most of all, his wife, Sarah.

T-REX TRYING AND TRYING...

The unfortunate trials of a modern prehistoric family.

Hugh Murphy

A PLUME BOOK

PLUME
Penguin Group (USA) LLC
375 Hudson Street
New York, New York 10014

USA | Canada | UK | Ireland | Australia | New Zealand | India | South Africa | China
penguin.com
A Penguin Random House Company

First published by Plume, a member of Penguin Group (USA) LLC, 2014

Copyright © 2014 by Hugh Murphy
Penguin supports copyright. Copyright fuels creativity, encourages diverse voices, promotes free speech, and creates a vibrant culture. Thank you for buying an authorized edition of this book and for complying with copyright laws by not reproducing, scanning, or distributing any part of it in any form without permission. You are supporting writers and allowing Penguin to continue to publish books for every reader.

Some illustrations previously appeared on the author's blog, http://trextrying.tumblr.com

REGISTERED TRADEMARK—MARCA REGISTRADA

ISBN 978-0-14-218170-6

Printed in the United States of America
10 9 8 7 6 5 4 3

Set in Ego Com Regular

For my family, the greatest source of inspiration, joy, and love in my life

T-Rex trying to put on a backpack . . .

T-Rex trying to reach his fanny pack . . .

T-Rex trying to go trick-or-treating . . .

T-Rex trying to use a magnifying glass . . .

T-Rex trying to use a pogo stick . . .

T-Rex trying to use a slingshot . . .

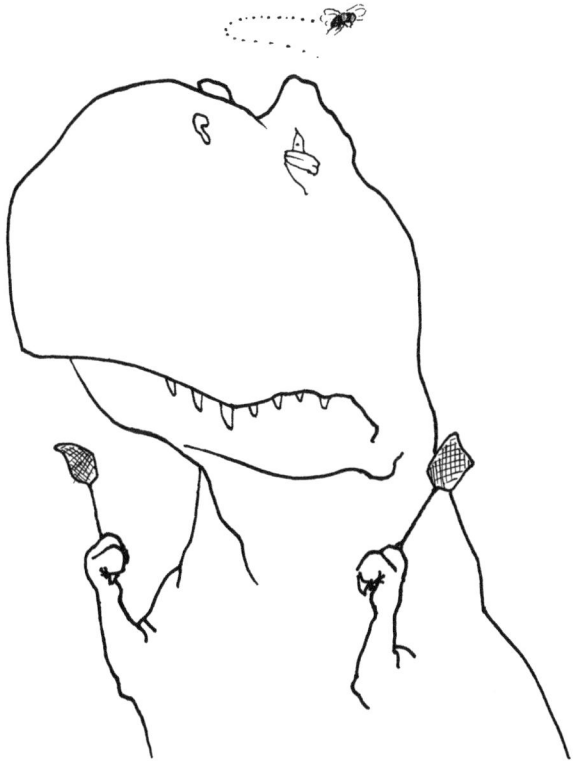

T-Rex trying to hurt a fly . . .

T-Rex trying to use chopsticks . . .

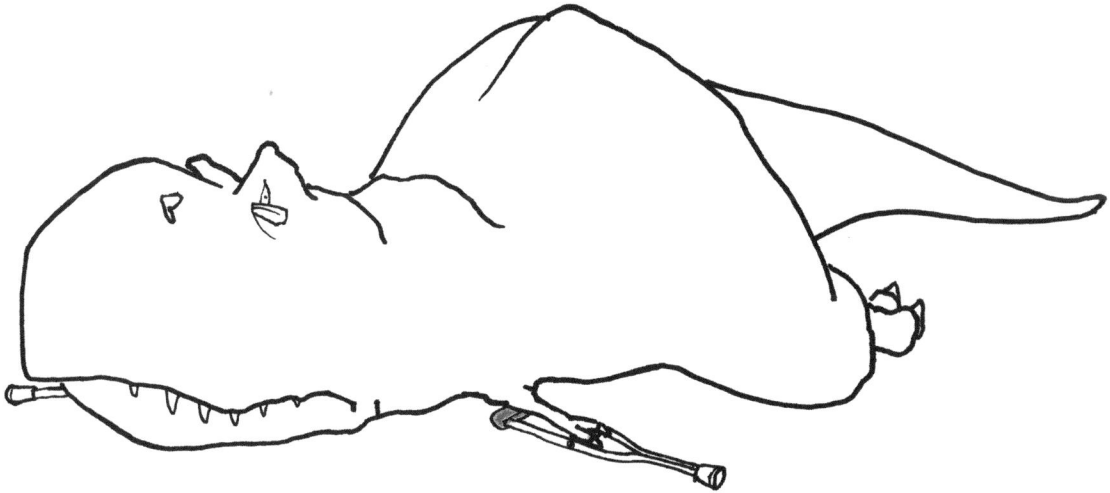

T-Rex trying to use crutches . . .

T-Rex trying to play the trombone . . .

T-Rex trying to control his jealousy . . .

T-Rex trying to bait a hook . . .

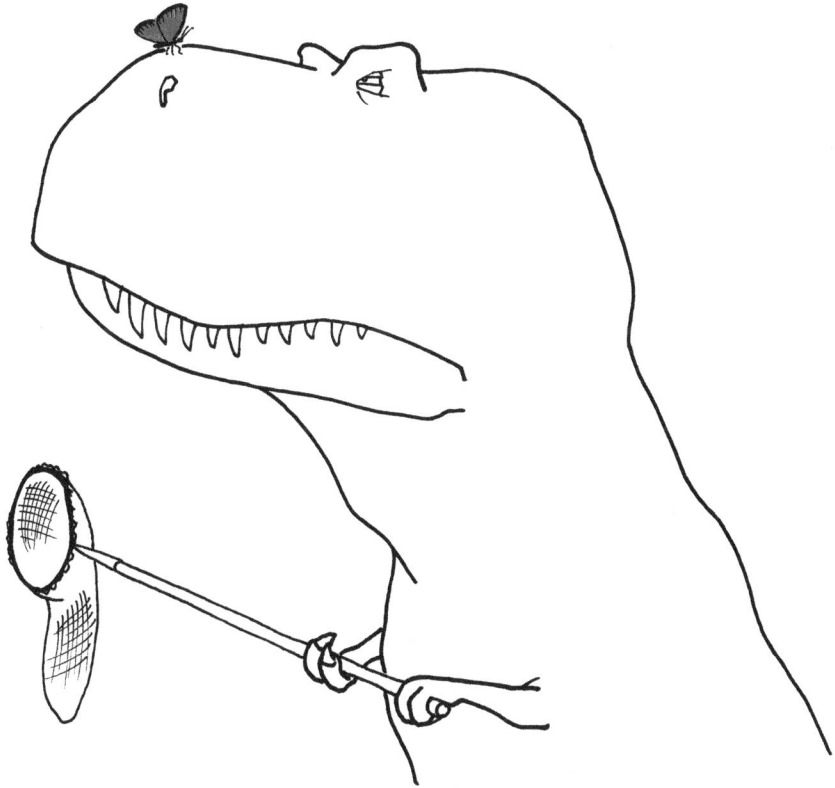

T-Rex trying to catch a butterfly . . .

T-Rex trying to bullfight . . .

T-Rex trying to blow a whistle . . .

T-Rex trying to surrender from a trench . . .

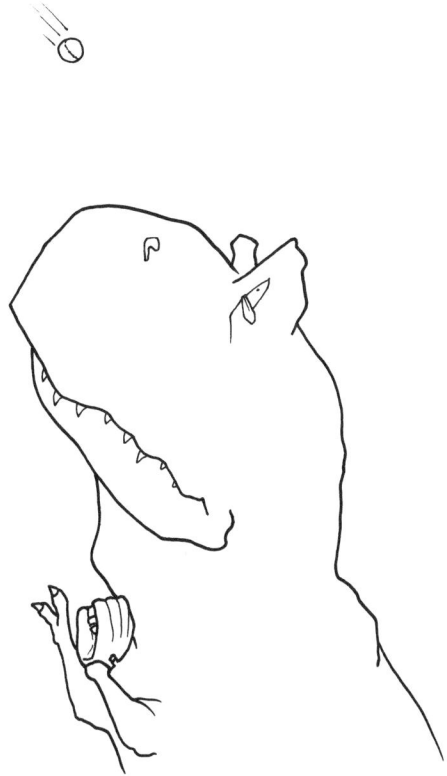

T-Rex trying to catch a fly ball . . .

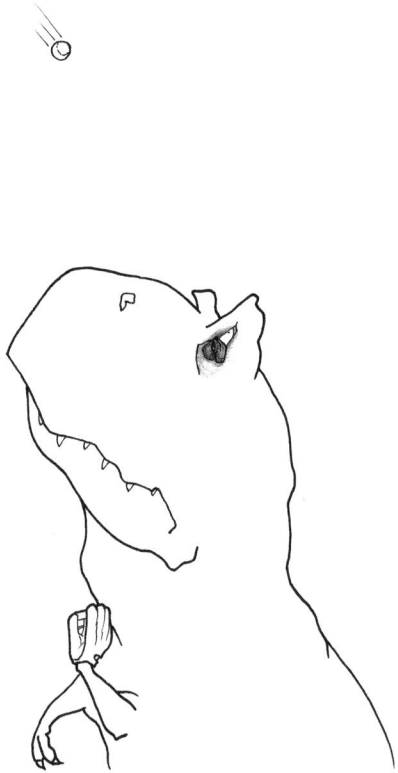

T-Rex trying to catch another fly ball . . .

T-Rex trying to challenge someone to a duel . . .

T-Rexes trying the biathlon . . .

T-Rex trying to hang his stocking . . .

T-Rexes trying to have a snowball fight . . .

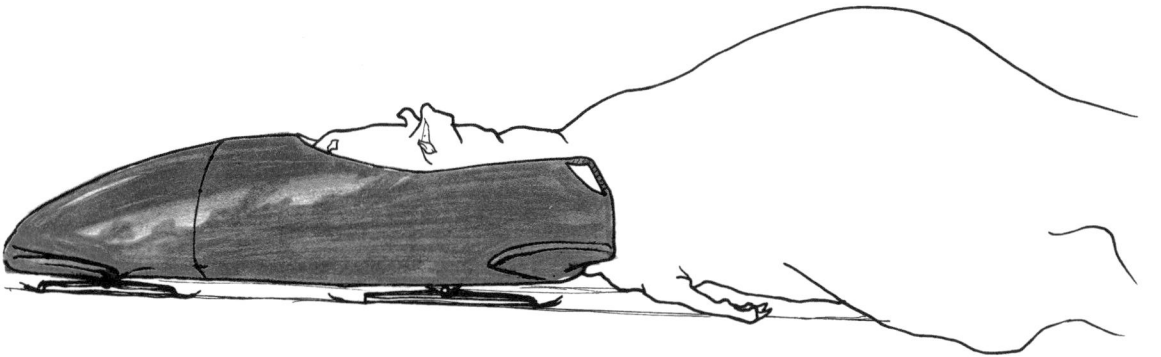

T-Rex trying to bobsled . . .

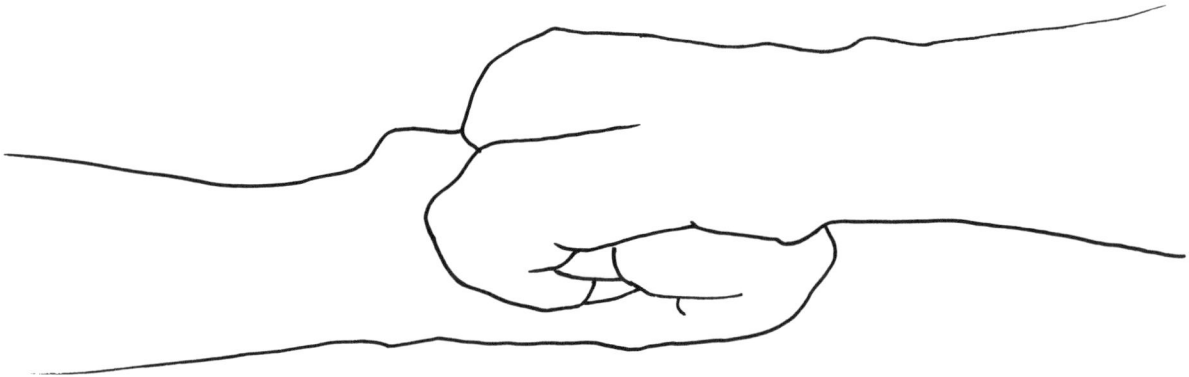

T-Rexes trying to thumb wrestle . . .

T-Rexes trying to pay the check . . .

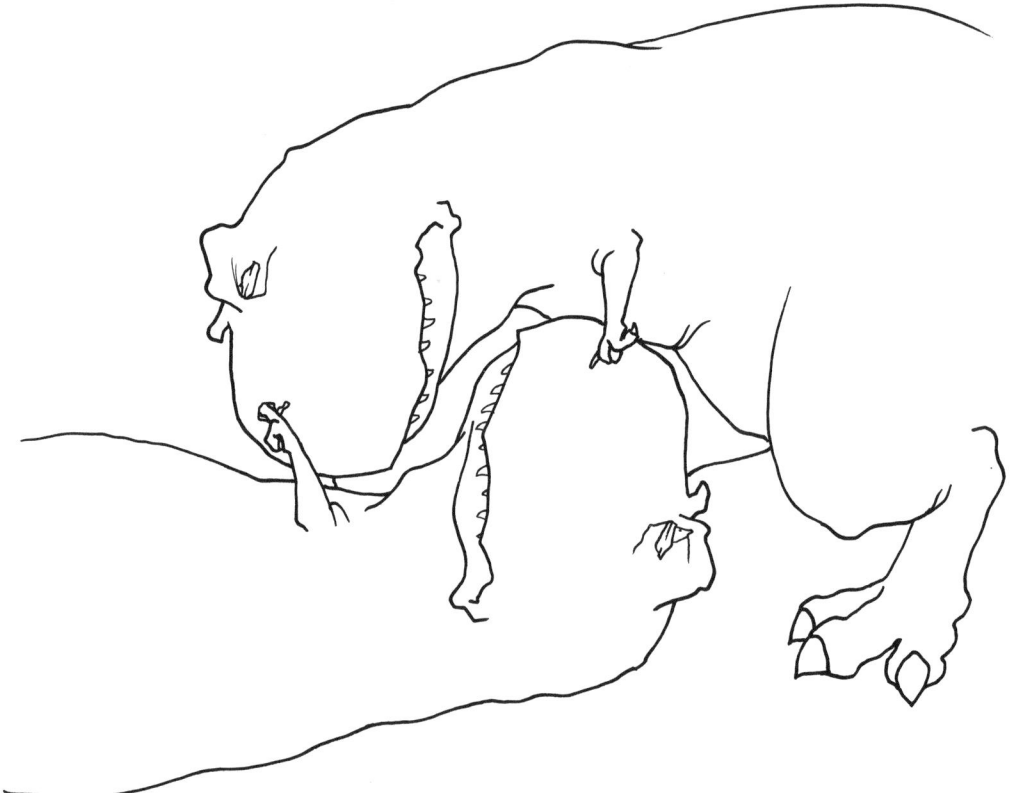

T-Rexes trying to pick their noses . . .

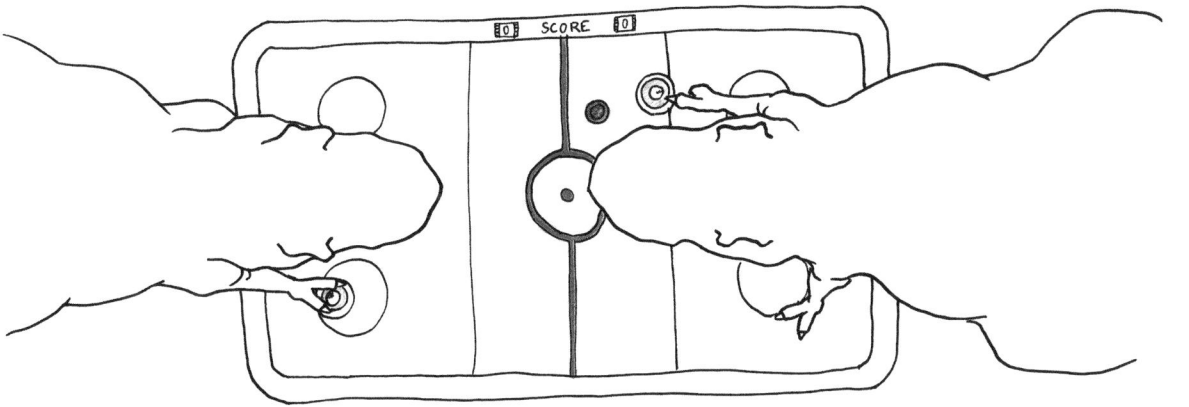

T-Rexes trying to play air hockey . . .

T-Rexes trying to play chess . . .

T-Rex trying to drink from a water fountain . . .

T-Rex trying to eat a lollipop . . .

T-Rex trying to eat corn on the cob . . .

T-Rex trying to fan away a fart . . .

T-Rex trying to find the light switch . . .

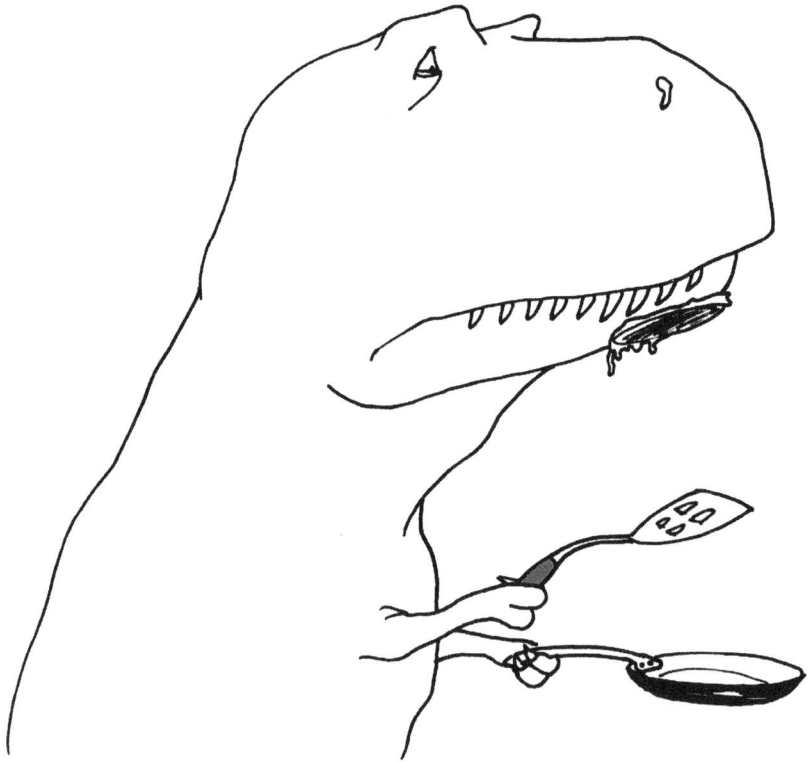

T-Rex trying to flip a pancake . . .

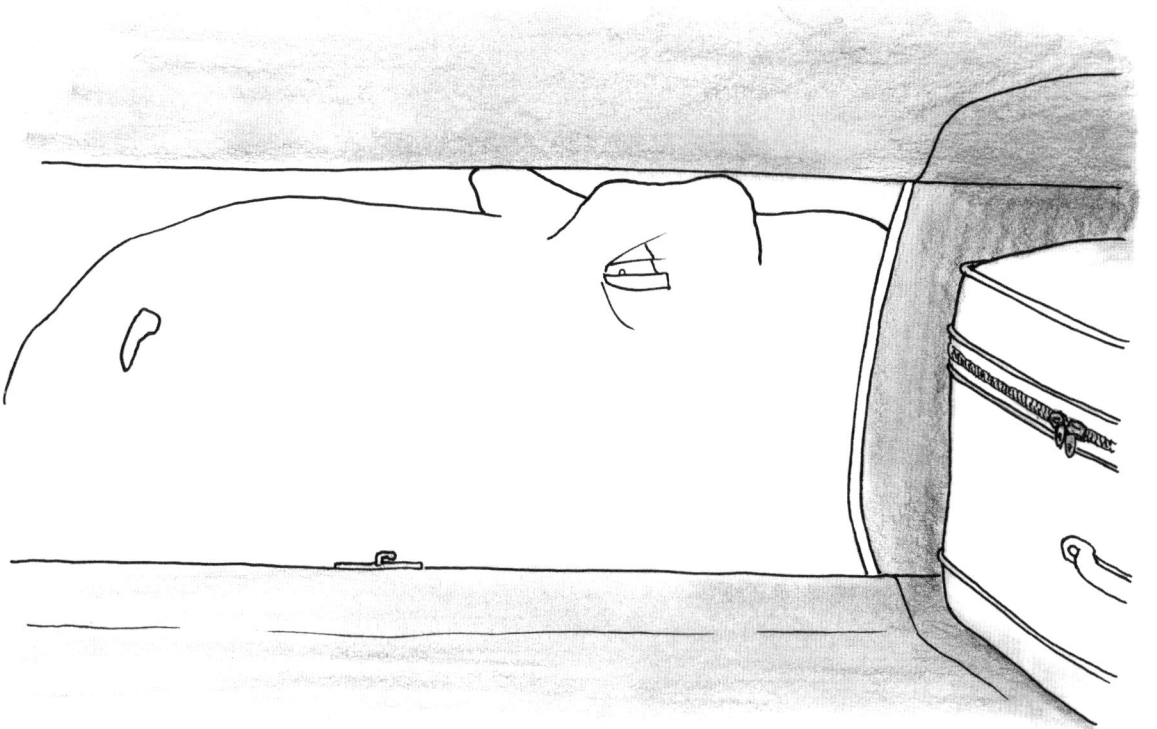

T-Rex trying to stow his bag in the overhead compartment . . .

T-Rex trying to eat dinner on an international flight . . .

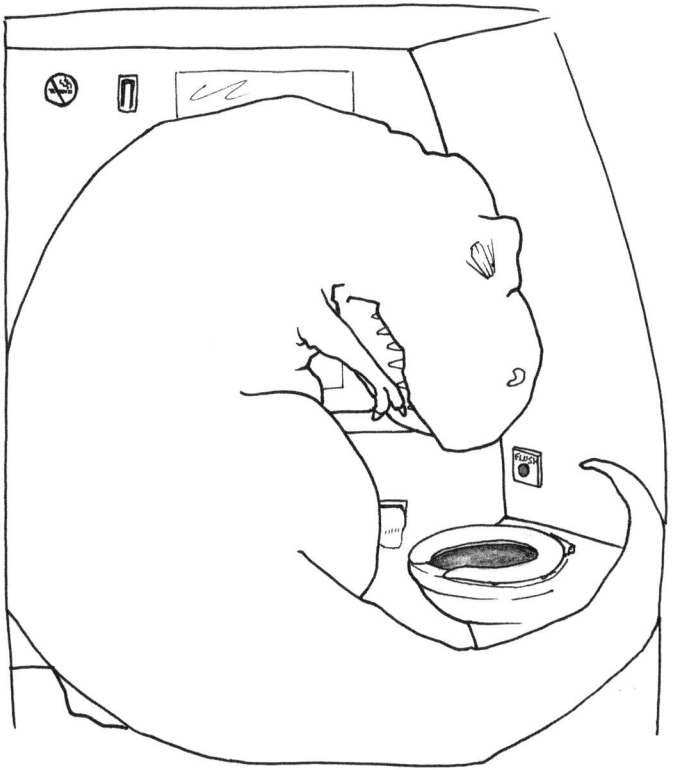

T-Rex trying to flush an airplane toilet . . .

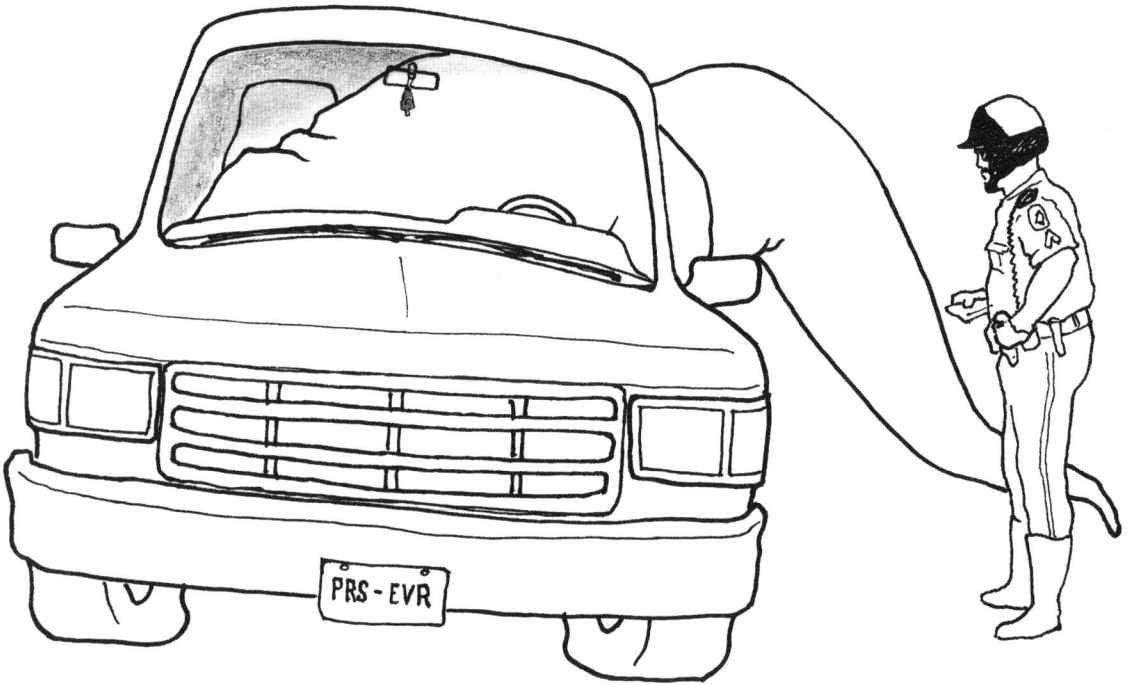

T-Rex trying to get his license and registration . . .

T-Rex trying to guide a plane to its gate . . .

T-Rex trying to help an old lady cross the street . . .

T-Rex trying to toot his own horn . . .

T-Rex trying to hike a football . . .

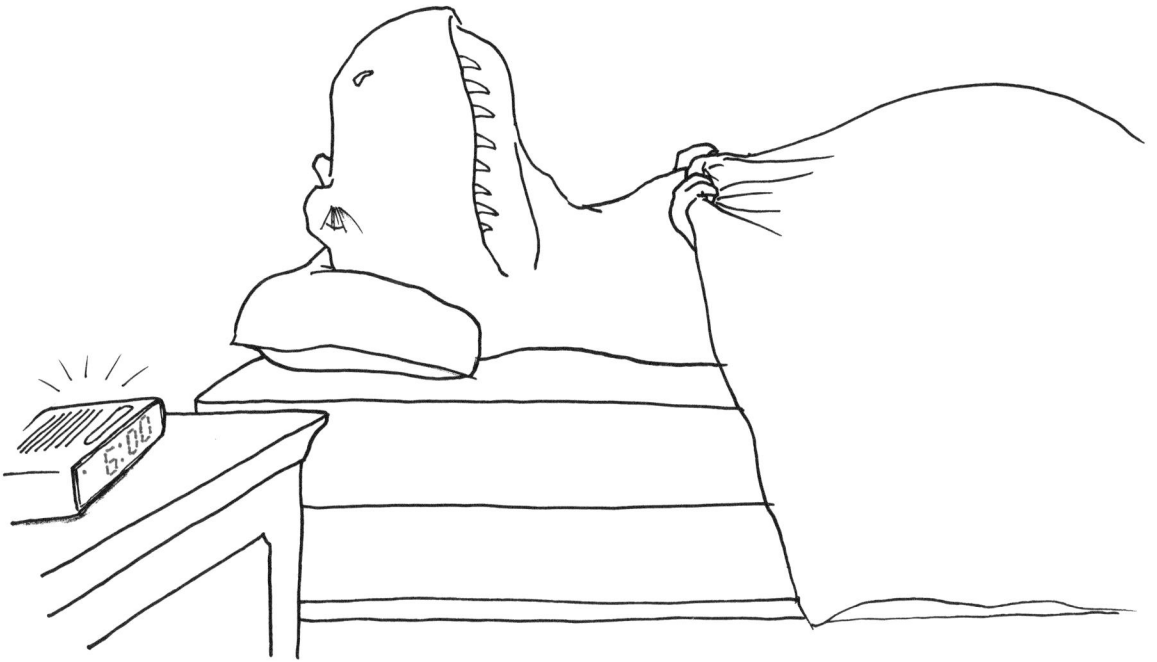

T-Rex trying to hit the snooze button . . .

T-Rex trying to hold hands with She-Rex . . .

T-Rex trying to use a Hula-Hoop . . .

T-Rex trying to loofah his back . . .

T-Rex trying to make shadow puppets . . .

T-Rex trying to use a weed whacker . . .

T-Rex trying to use a wheelbarrow . . .

T-Rex trying to landscape . . .

T-Rex trying to clean the lint out of his belly button . . .

T-Rex trying to measure his inseam . . .

She-Rex trying to Nair her legs . . .

She-Rex trying to paint her toenails . . .

She-Rex trying to put on a bra . . .

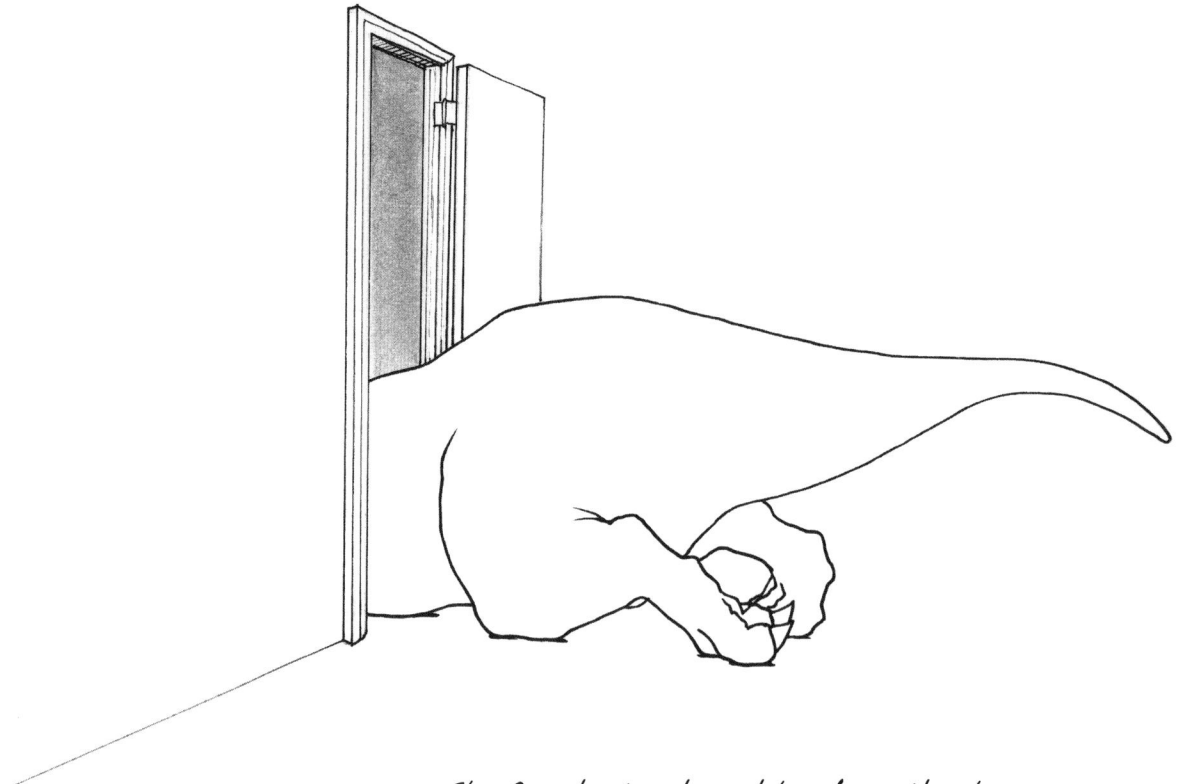

She-Rex trying to get her favorite shoes . . .

She-Rex trying to put on eye shadow . . .

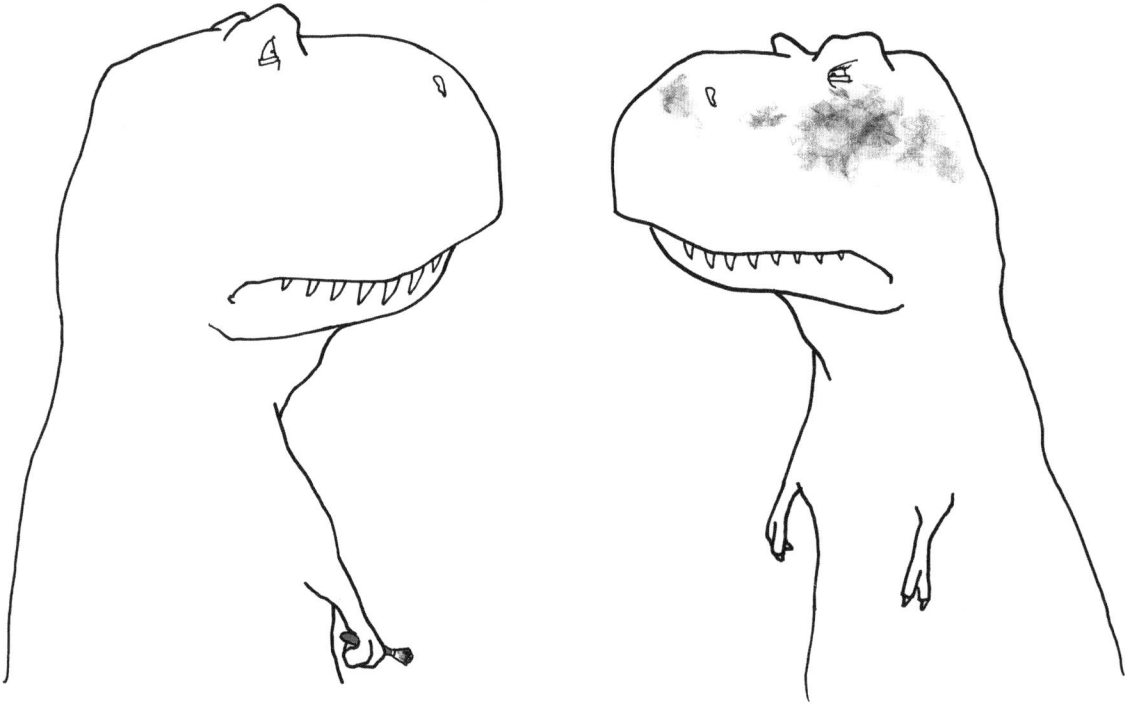

T-Rex trying to help She-Rex put on eye shadow . . .

She-Rex trying to find her keys in her purse . . .

She-Rex trying to get her stiletto repaired . . .

T-Rex trying to dip his dance partner . . .

T-Rex trying to grab a cab for She-Rex . . .

T-Rex trying to open the door for She-Rex . . .

T-Rex trying to pour She-Rex a glass of wine . . .

She-Rex trying to catch the bouquet at a wedding . . .

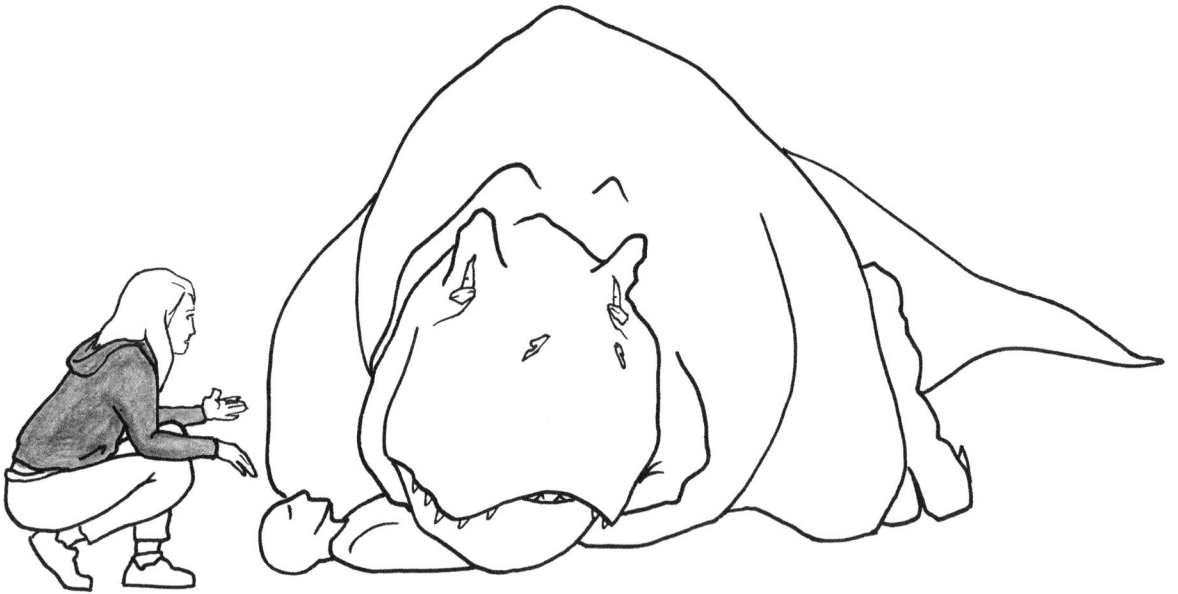

T-Rex trying to learn CPR . . .

T-Rex trying to tell everyone he's choking . . .

She-Rex trying to perform the Heimlich on T-Rex . . .

T-Rex trying to grab the low-hanging fruit . . .

T-Rex trying to fit in . . .

T-Rex trying to reconnect . . .

T-Rex trying to settle an old score . . .

T-Rex trying to raise awareness for prehistoric extinctions . . .

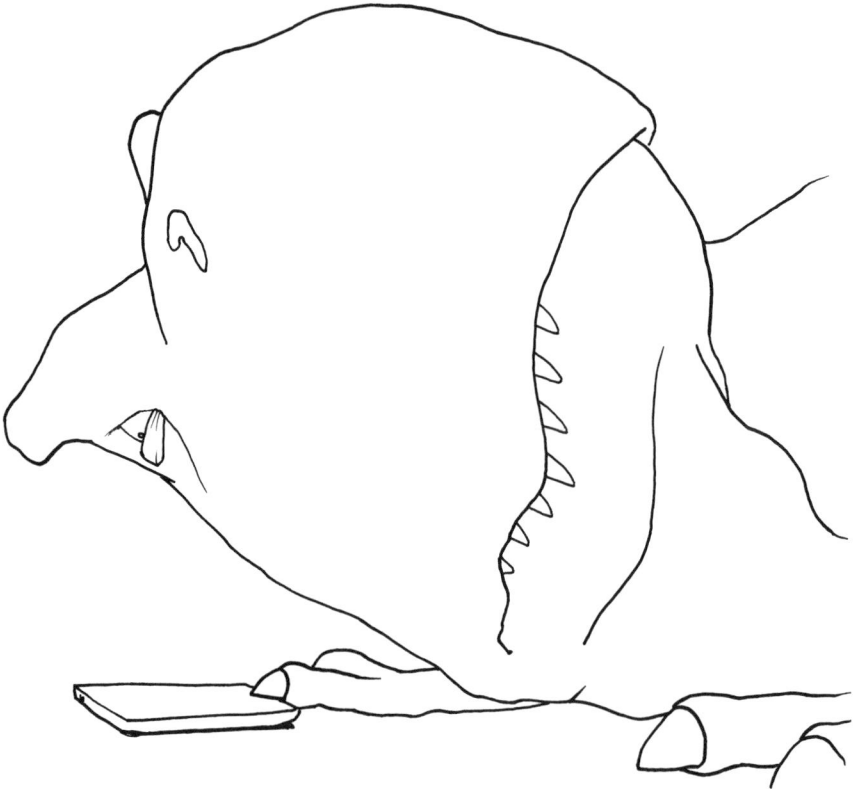

T-Rex trying to read his e-mail . . .

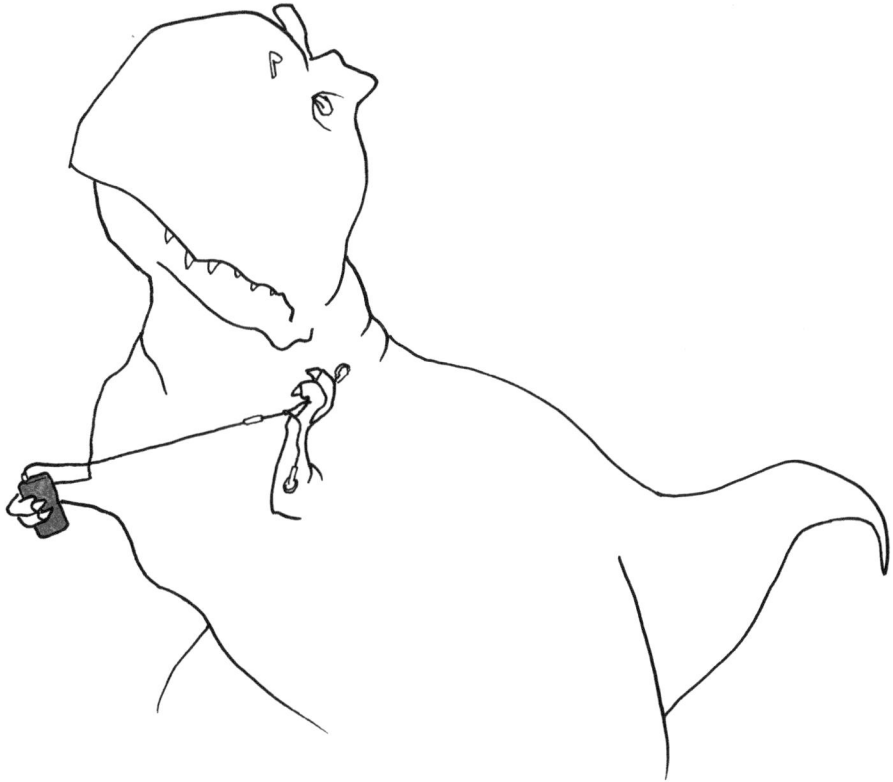

T-Rex trying to use a hands-free headset . . .

T-Rex trying to weather the stomach flu . . .

T-Rex trying to play Rock 'em Sock 'em Robots . . .

T-Rex trying to set a mousetrap . . .

T-Rex trying to shave . . .

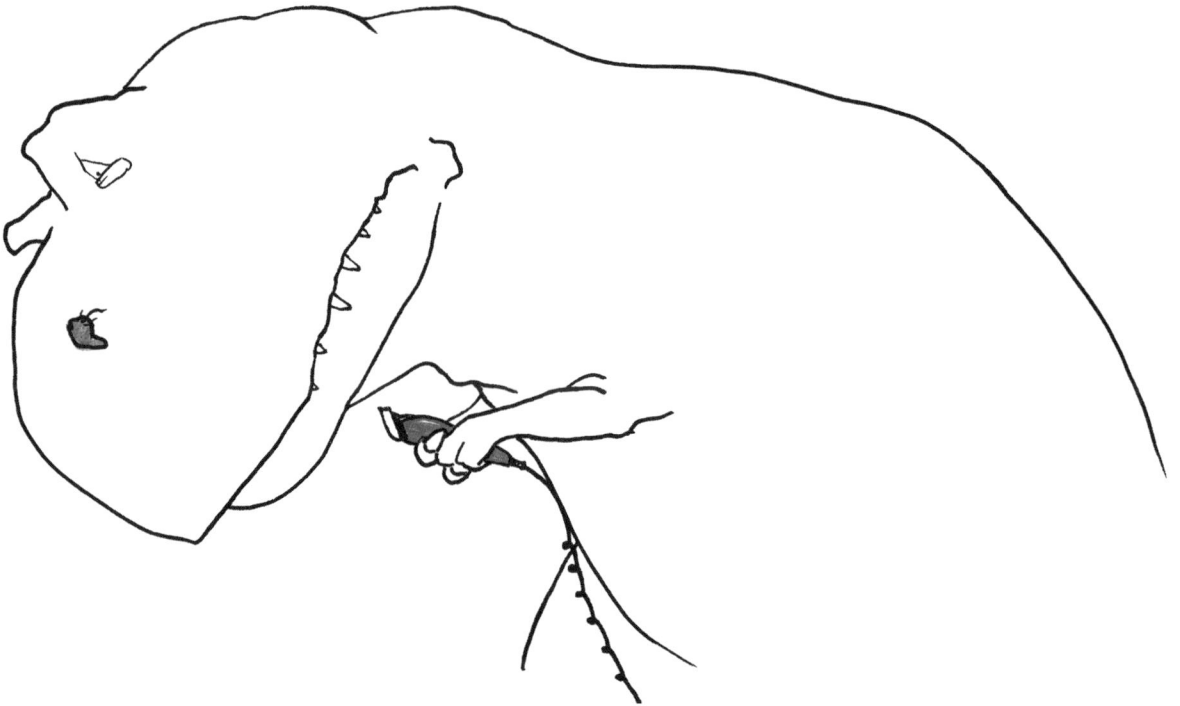

T-Rex trying to trim his nose hairs . . .

T-Rex trying to make a move while watching a movie . . .

T-Rex trying to spoon She-Rex . . .

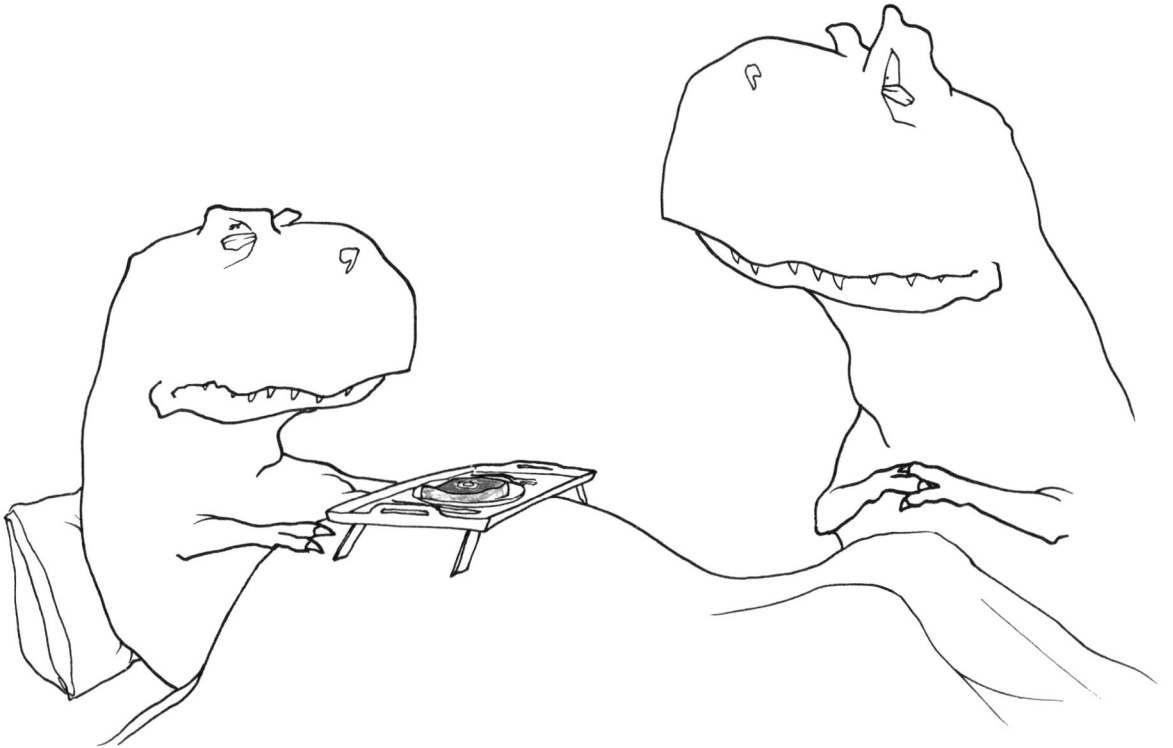

T-Rex trying to serve She-Rex breakfast in bed . . .

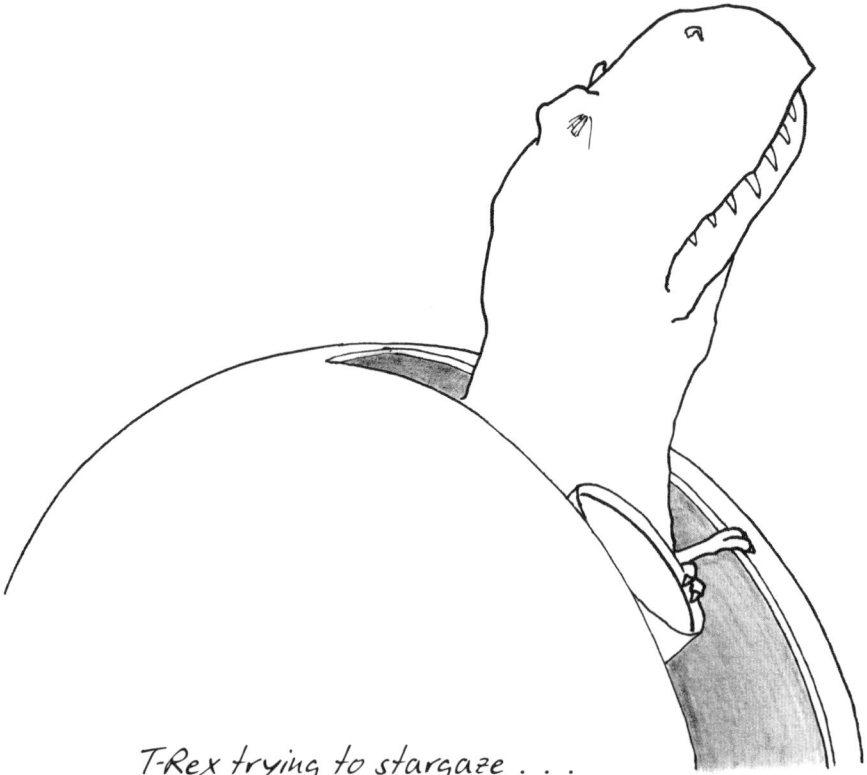

T-Rex trying to stargaze . . .

T-Rex trying to take a face-off . . .

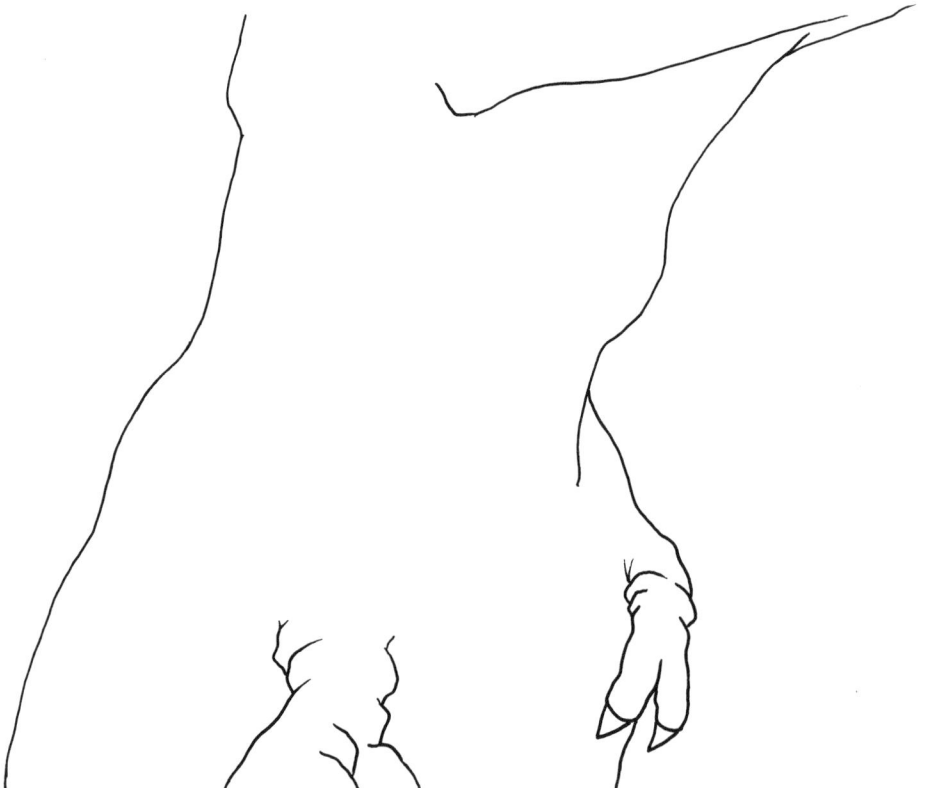

T-Rex trying to take a selfie . . .

T-Rex trying to get something special for She-Rex . . .

T-Rex trying to teach She-Rex how to make pottery . . .

T-Rex trying to propose to She-Rex . . .

T-Rex trying to toast with She-Rex . . .

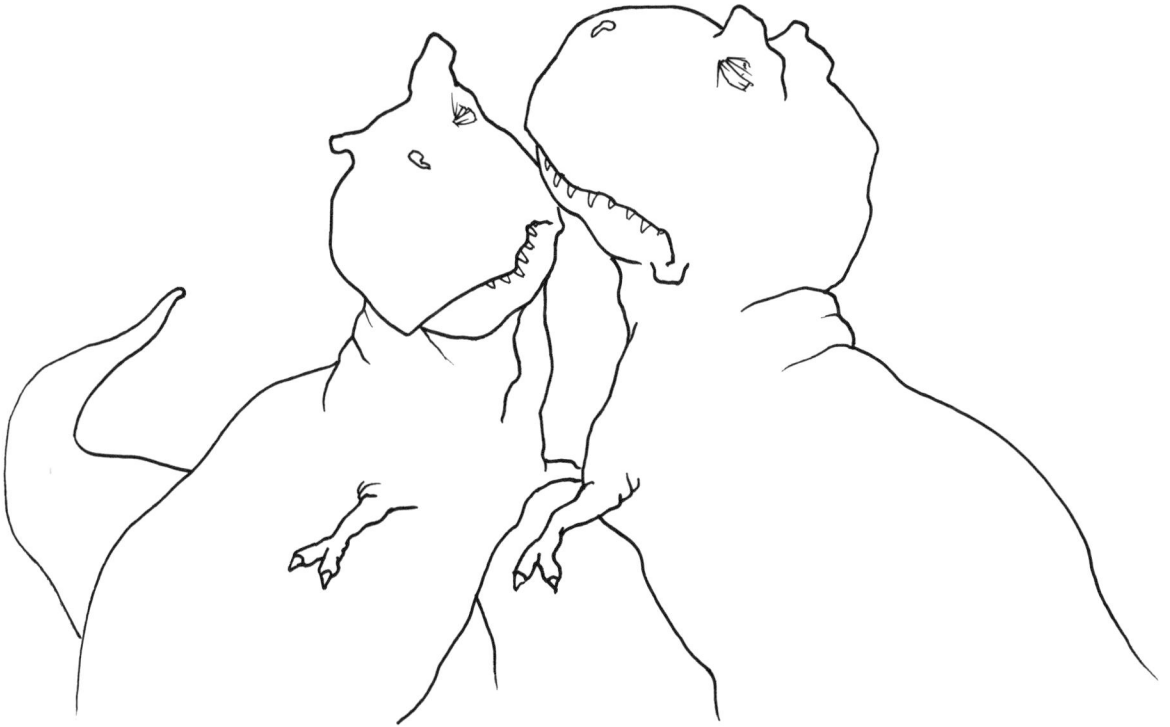

T-Rexes trying to chest bump . . .

T-Rex trying to carry She-Rex across the threshold . . .

T-Rex trying to vault . . .

T-Rex trying to win a sack race . . .

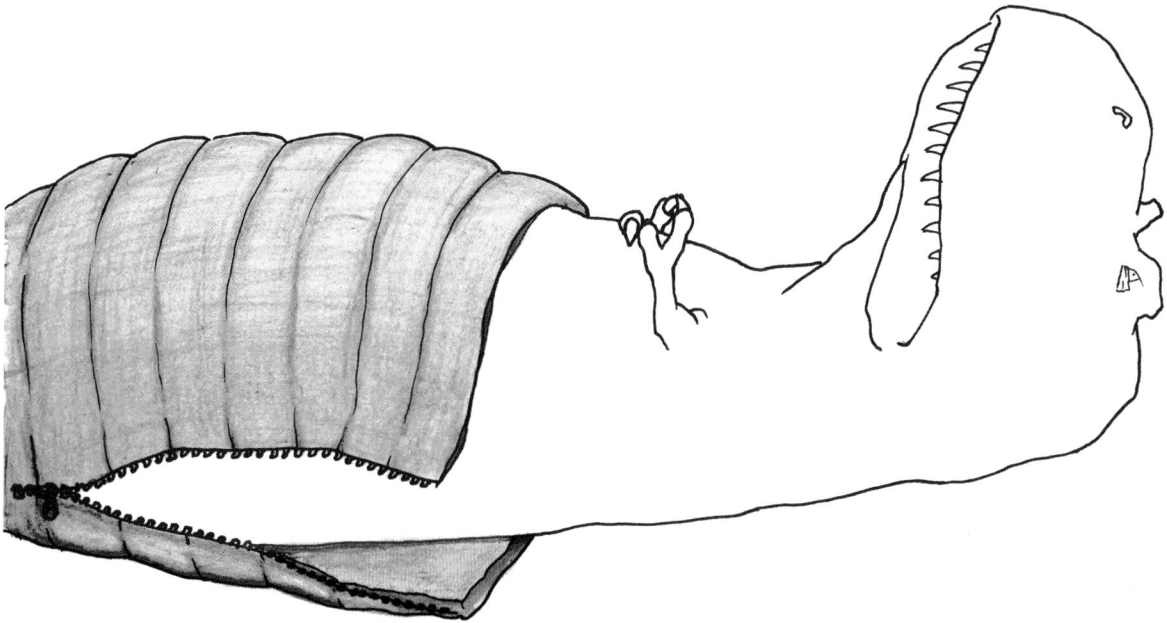

T-Rex trying to zip up his sleeping bag . . .

T-Rex trying to shovel his driveway . . .

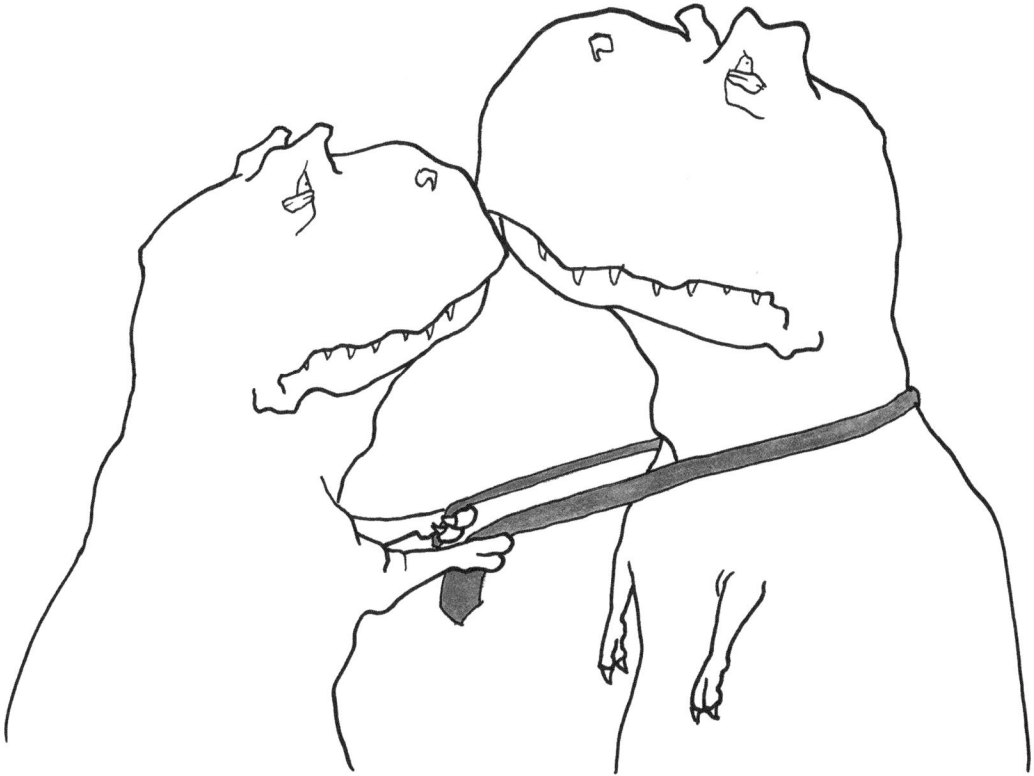

She-Rex trying to help T-Rex with his tie . . .

She-Rex trying to help T-Rex with his tie . . .

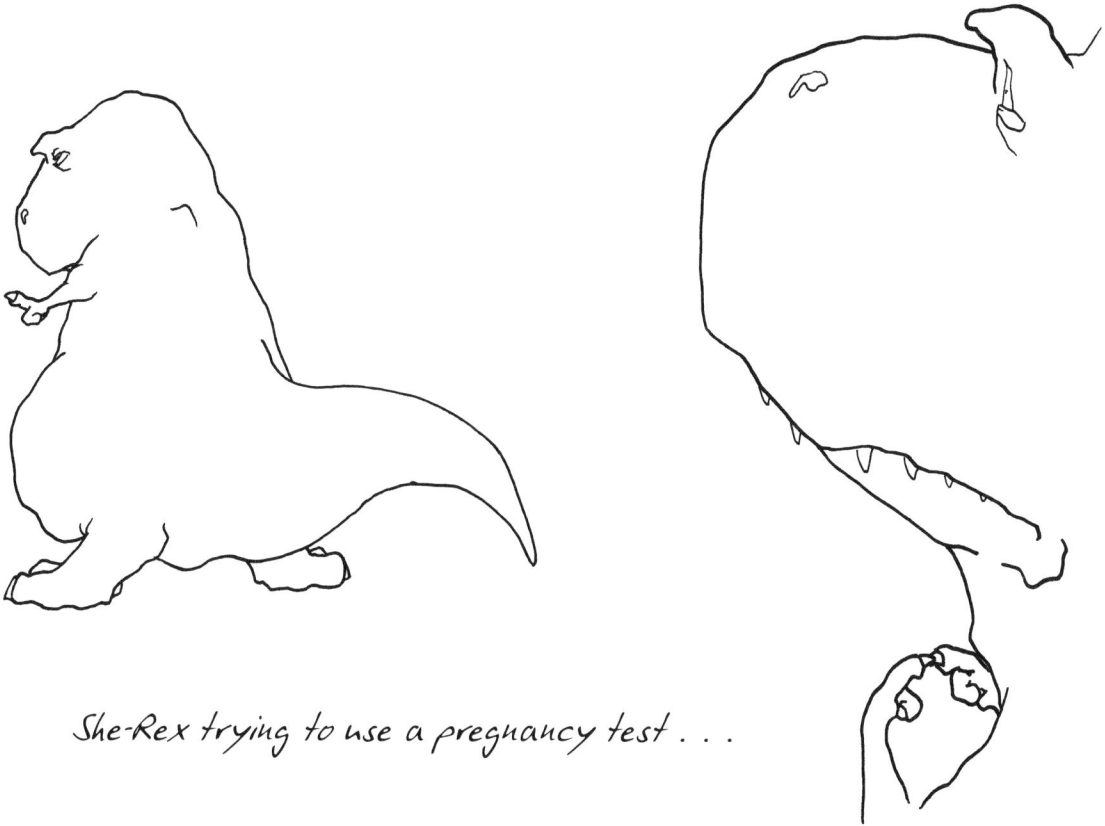

She-Rex trying to use a pregnancy test . . .

She-Rex trying to lower T-Rex's cholesterol . . .

T-Rex trying to deliver Wee-Rex . . .

T-Rex and She-Rex trying to shop for car seats . . .

T-Rex trying to get Wee-Rex out of his crib . . .

T-Rex trying to change Wee-Rex's diaper . . .

T-Rex trying to change Wee-Rex's diaper . . .

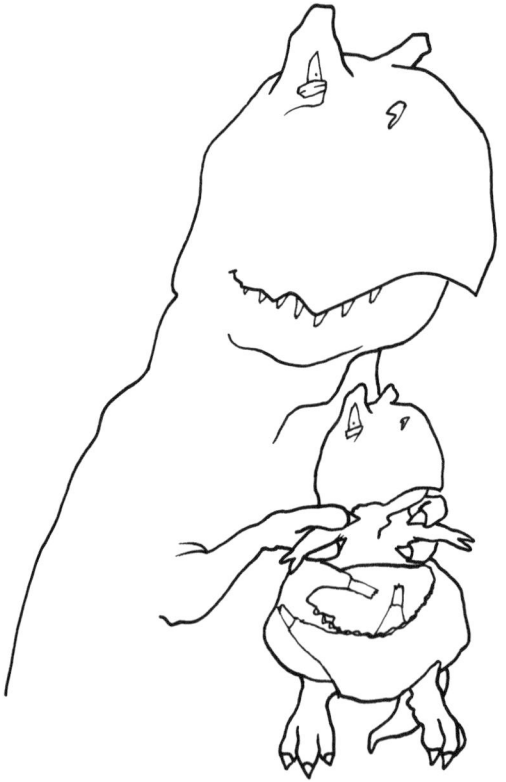

T-Rex trying to change Wee-Rex's diaper . . .

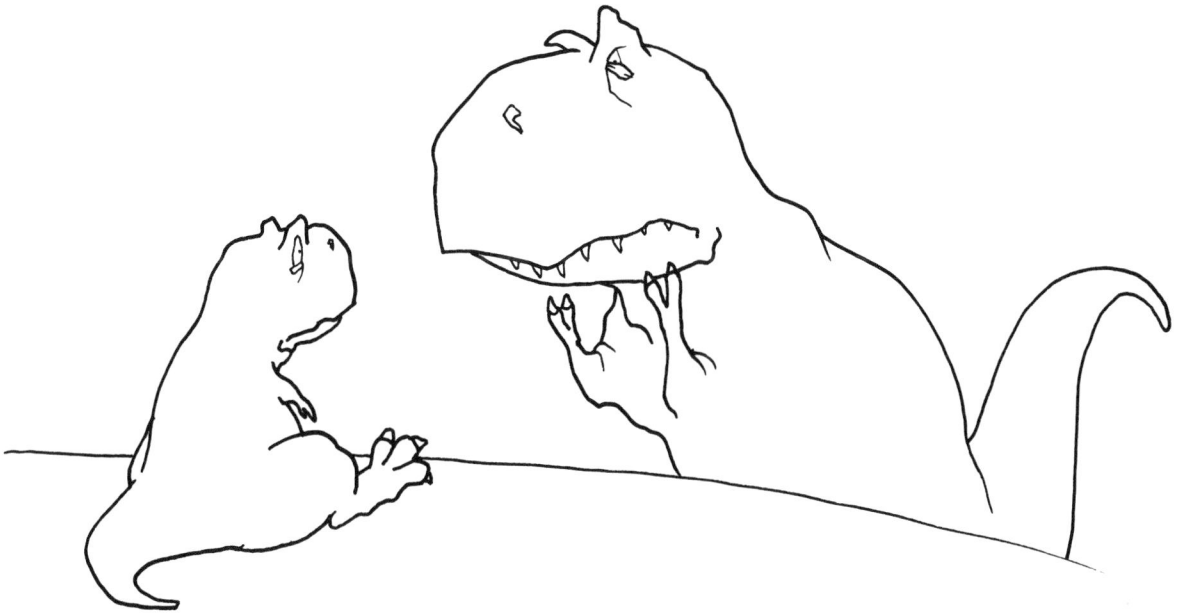

T-Rex trying to play peek-a-boo with Wee-Rex . . .

T-Rex trying to install a car seat . . .

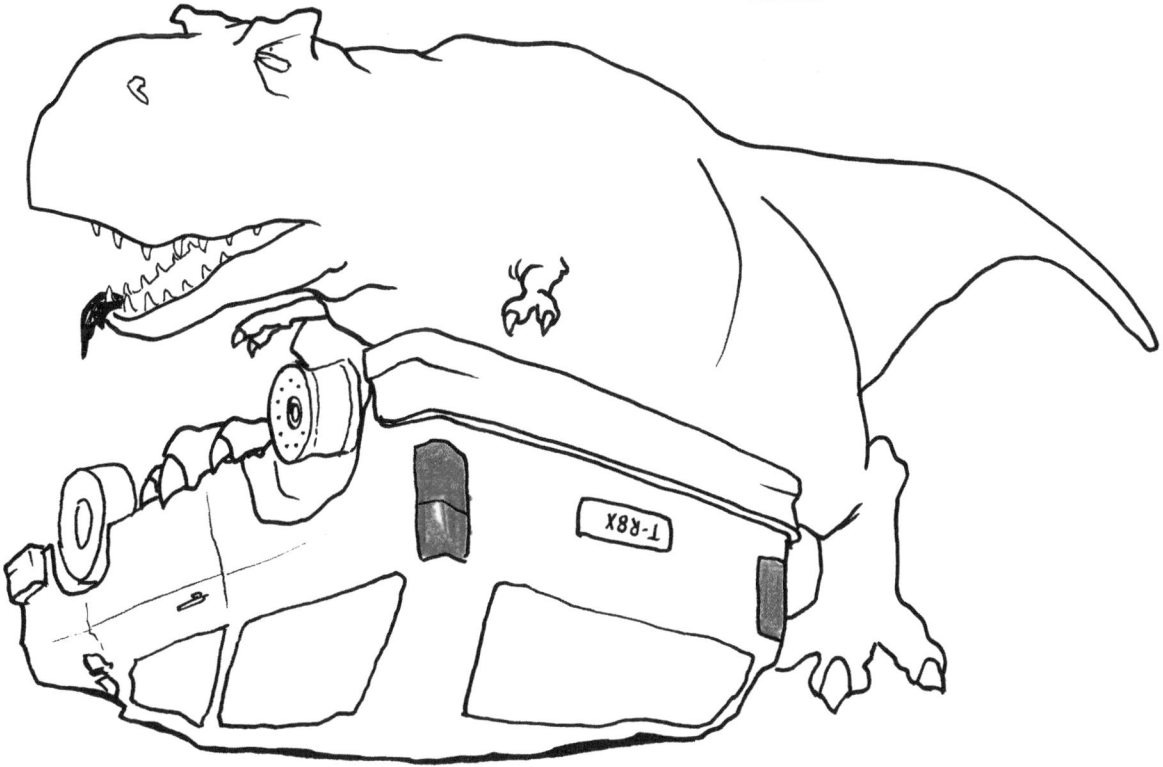

T-Rex trying to change a tire . . .

Wee-Rex trying to crawl . . .

Wee-Rex trying to use his new power wheels . . . Big Wheel . . . ROLLERBLADES!!!

Wee-Rex trying to finger paint . . .

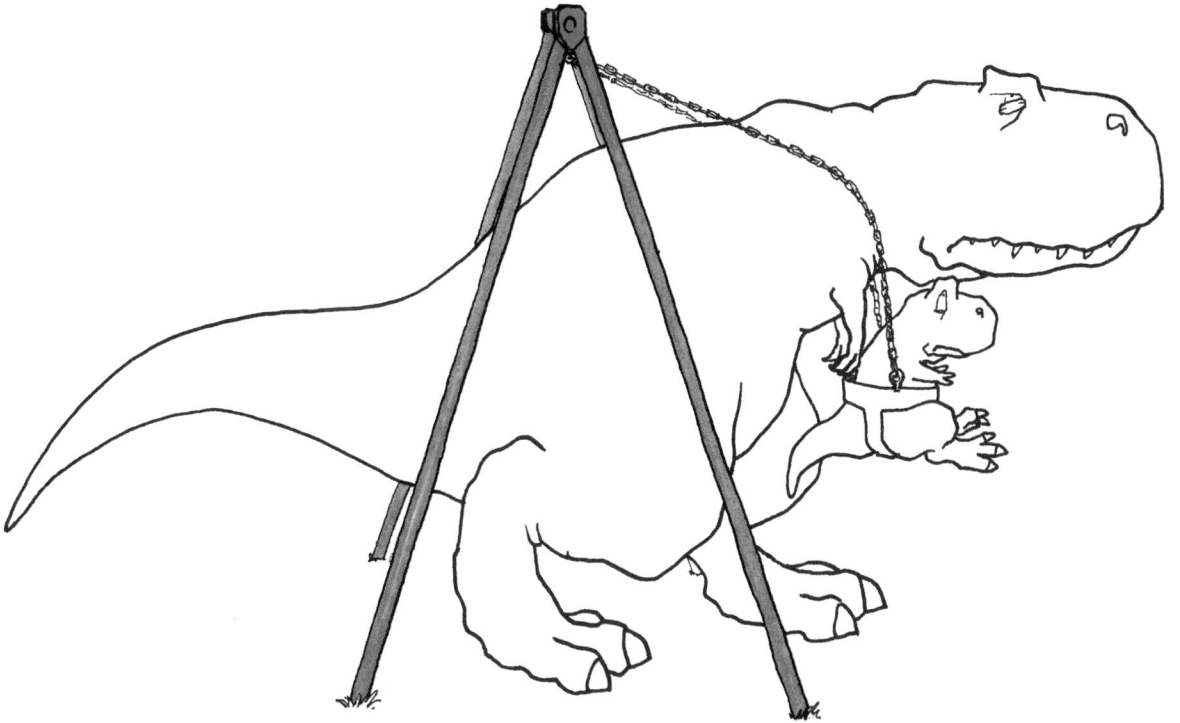

T-Rex trying to push Wee-Rex on a swing . . .

T-Rex trying to give She-Rex a gift . . .

T-Rex trying to explain where wee-rexes come from . . .

Wee-Rex trying to play dodgeball . . .

Wee-Rex trying to play with his toys in the bath . . .

T-Rex and Wee-Rex trying to pitch a tent . . .

T-Rex trying to put on his dentures . . .

T-Rex trying to see what's so funny . . .

T-Rex trying to be cool about it . . .

T-Rex trying to preserve his dignity . . .